This book belongs to:

_____

_____

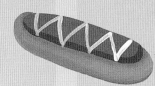

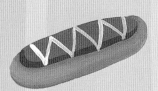

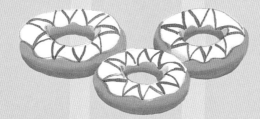

tiger tales
5 River Road, Suite 128, Wilton, CT 06897
Published in the United States 2016
Originally published in Great Britain 2014
by Little Tiger Press
Text copyright © 2014 Little Tiger Press
Illustrations copyright © 2014 Miriam Latimer

ISBN-13: 978-1-58925-477-0
ISBN-10: 1-58925-477-5
Printed in China
LTP/1400/1268/0815
All rights reserved
10 9 8 7 6 5 4 3 2 1

For more insight and activities, visit us at
www.tigertalesbooks.com

To Katie and Sarah—we make
the tastiest gingerbread men
(and houses!) ~ M. A.

For Summer and Heidi xx
~ M. L.

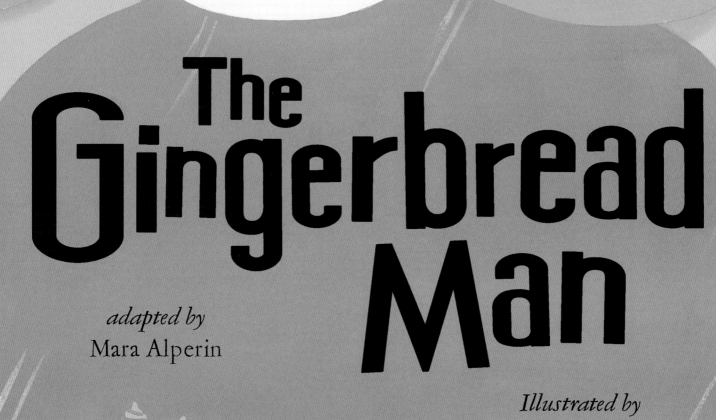

The Gingerbread Man

adapted by
Mara Alperin

Illustrated by
Miriam Latimer

tiger tales

Mr. and Mrs. Baker lived all alone. Day after day, they baked big gooey cakes, sweet crumbly pies, and piping hot pastries. But they had no one to share them with, and that made them very sad.

Then one day, Mrs. Baker made a little gingerbread man
to cheer them both up. He had jolly jelly buttons
and a big icing smile. Dusting the flour from her hands,
she popped him into the oven . . . .

But to Mr. and Mrs. Baker's surprise, when the tray came out, the gingerbread man leaped up onto the table, and began skipping through the sugar!

"Tee hee hee! You can't catch me!" he giggled.

"Bless my cinnamon stars!" cried Mrs. Baker as they chased him over pots, under pans, and all around the kitchen . . . .

But the gingerbread man was too quick for them, and he **jumped** right out the window!

Scurrying along the path,
the gingerbread man ran into
a **very hungry** cow.
"You look **tasty**," mooed
the cow. "And what fine jelly
buttons you have!"

But the gingerbread man just
danced and pranced, singing,

"Run, run,
as fast as you can!
You can't catch me.
I'm the gingerbread man!"

And off he ran — as fast as his
gingerbread legs could carry him!

With a great Mooo! the cow thundered
after the gingerbread man,
past the milk churns,

through the barn,

and around and around
the haystack, until . . .

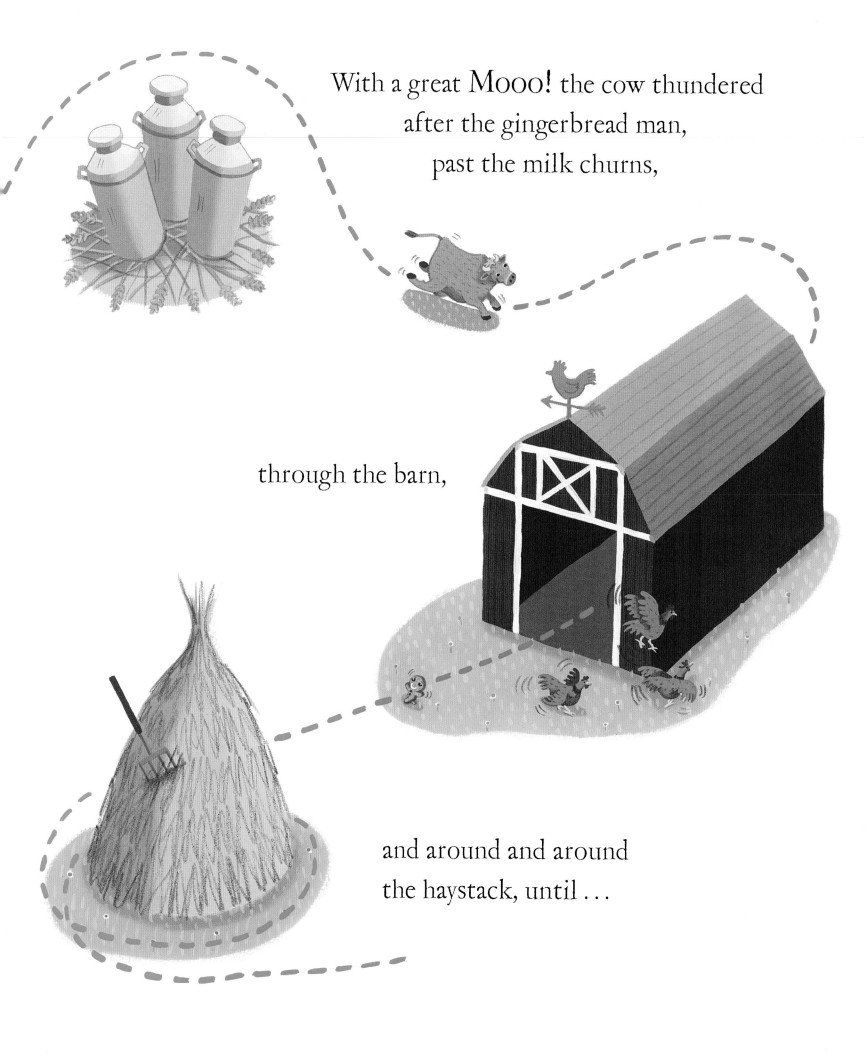

CRASH!
The haystack tumbled over,
right on top of
the cow!

"Oh, milkshakes!" cried the
very dizzy cow.

The gingerbread man scampered up the hill.
At the top was a **very hungry** goat.
"Good day," bleated the goat.
"I **love** munching thistles, but **you**
look even **better to eat**."

But the gingerbread man just whirled and twirled, singing,

"Run, run,
as fast as you can!
You can't catch me.
I'm the gingerbread man!"

And off he zoomed —
leaving a trail of gingerbread
crumbs behind him!

So the goat dashed after the gingerbread man, through the thistles,

over the gate,

and in and out of the apple orchard, until ...

SMASH!

The goat butted right
into a tree and the
apples came
toppling
down
with a

thud!

thud!
thud!

"Oh, applesauce!" cried the goat,
rubbing his head.

"Tee hee hee," laughed the gingerbread man, as he frolicked through the meadow. There, dozing in a tree, was a **very hungry** cat.

"Hello," meowed the cat. "You look like the **purr-fect** snack!"

But the gingerbread man just
wiggled and giggled, singing,

"Run, run,
as fast as you can!
You can't catch me.
I'm the gingerbread man!"

And off he whooshed — racing down
the lane!

Licking her lips, the cat chased the gingerbread man, around the bush,

through the daisies,
and toward the pond.

The cat leaped up, up, up...

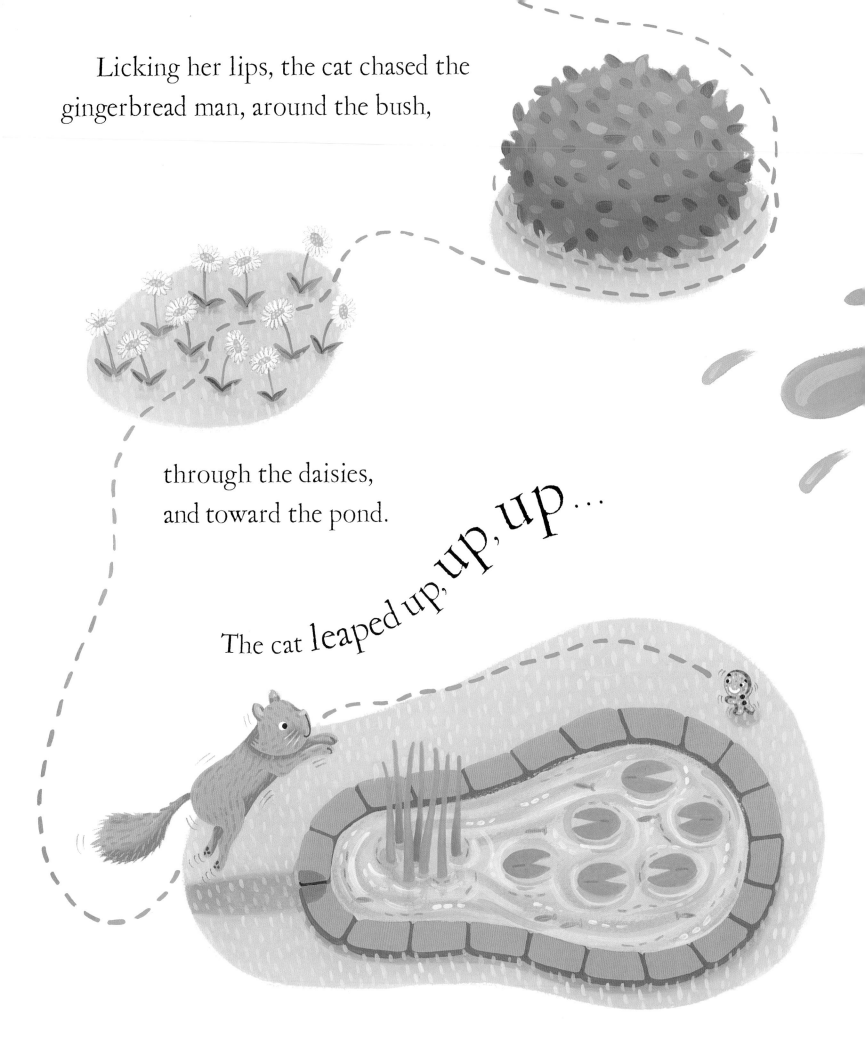

and came down,
down,
down...
SPLASH!
right in the middle of the
cold, wet pond!

"Oh, whiskers!" grumbled
the very soggy cat.

As the gingerbread man
ran down the hill, he began
to laugh and sing,

"Tee hee hee! I'm having fun!
I've run away from everyone!
A curly-haired woman,
A man in a hat,
A cow and a goat,
And a silly old cat!"

But when the gingerbread man reached
the riverbank, he stopped and shivered.

"Brrr, too cold! How
do I cross?"

Just then, a fox appeared.
"Hello, little gingerbread man,"
he grinned. "Maybe I can help you.
Just climb on my tail, and I'll
carry you across."

"Brrr, too chilly!" the gingerbread man squealed, as the fox paddled into the river.

"Then why don't you climb onto my back?" asked the fox.

"Brrr, too wet!" squeaked the gingerbread man, as the water swirled at his feet.

"Climb onto my head," smirked the fox, and the gingerbread man scrambled up.

But the water rose higher still, so the gingerbread man climbed to the top of the fox's nose.

"Tee hee hee! They'll never catch me!"

he cried, just as . . .

...the fox tossed the gingerbread man up, up, UP in the air and opened his mouth w i d e ...

SNAP!

And that was the end of the gingerbread man!

"Oh, dear," sighed Mrs. Baker. "What a naughty gingerbread man he was."

"I'm still hungry!" mooed the cow.
"Me too-oo," bleated the goat.
"So am I," meowed the cat.

Then Mr. Baker said, "Let's all go and bake something else together!"

So they all trotted back to the bakery to mix and stir cakes and pastries and pies . . . but no more gingerbread men! It was a **fantastic feast**, and with their three new friends, Mr. and Mrs. Baker were **never** lonely again!

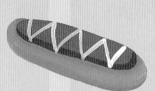

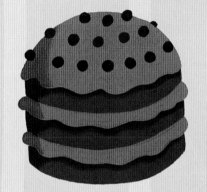

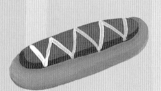

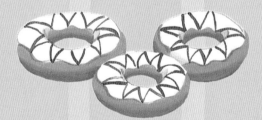